MY LITTLE CAR

Gary Soto

ILLUSTRATED BY

Pam Paparone

G. P. PUTNAM'S SONS

To Josie Rangel and Juan Garcia

Lowriding in Clovis, California.—G. S.

For Nick.—P. P.

Abuelito • grandfather

¡Bailelo! • Make it dance!

carrito • little car

chile • chili pepper

con cariño • with affection

Es mi carrito. • It's my car.

¡Híjole! • Gosh! Wow!

mi • my

mi'ja • my daughter (affectionately)

muchacha • girl

muy firme • really good-looking

pues • well

querida • dear, beloved

ranfla • low-riding car

Sí, es la verdad. • Yes, it's true.

también • also

G. P. PUTNAM'S SONS

A division of Penguin Young Readers Group. Published by The Penguin Group. Penguin Group (USA) Inc., 375 Hudson Street, New York, NY 10014, U.S.A. Penguin Group (Canada), 90 Eglinton Avenue East, Toronto, Ontario, Canada M4P 2Y3 (a division of Pearson Penguin Canada Inc.). Penguin Books Ltd, 80 Strand, London WC2R 0RL, England. Penguin Ireland, 25 St. Stephen's Green, Dublin 2, Ireland (a division of Penguin Books Ltd.). Penguin Group (Australia), 250 Camberwell Road, Camberwell, Victoria 3124, Australia (a division of Pearson Australia Group Pty Ltd). Penguin Books India Pvt Ltd, 11 Community Centre, Panchsheel Park, New Delhi - 110 017, India. Penguin Group (NZ), Cnr Airborne and Rosedale Roads, Albany, Auckland 1310, New Zealand (a division of Pearson New Zealand Ltd). Penguin Books (South Africa) (Pty) Ltd, 24 Studee Avenue, Rosebank, Johannesburg 2196, South Africa. Penguin Books Ltd, Registered Offices: 80 Strand, London WC2R 0RL, England.

Published simultaneously in Canada. Manufactured in China by South China Printing Co. Ltd.

Design by Marikka Tamura. Text set in Usherwood Bold. The art was done in acrylic.

Library of Congress Cataloging-in-Publication Data

Soto, Gary. My little car / Gary Soto ; illustrated by Pam Paparone. p. cm. Summary: Teresa loves to show off her shiny, new, pedal-powered lowrider car from Grandpa, but the toy soon looks old when she neglects it. [1. Lowriders—Fiction. 2. Responsibility—Fiction. 3. Automobiles—Fiction. 4. Toys—Fiction. 5. Grandfathers—Fiction. 6. Mexican Americans—Fiction.] I. Paparone, Pamela, ill. II. Title. PZ7.S7242 2006 [E]—dc21 98-042826 ISBN 0-399-23220-6

1 3 5 7 9 10 8 6 4 2

First Impression

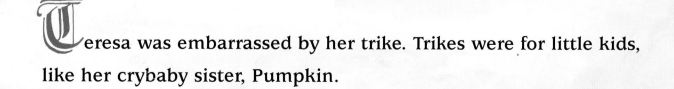

Teresa was embarrassed by her trike. Trikes were for little kids,
like her crybaby sister, Pumpkin.

Then the mailman delivered a big birthday present from *Abuelito* Benito.

"Can I open it?" Teresa asked her mother.

"Go for it, *mi'ja*," her mother said.

Teresa tore at the wrapping with her fingernails.

"It's a lowrider," Teresa cried. "Look at the flames!"

Her mother read the card from her grandfather:

"*Querida* Teresita: You're old enough for your first lowrider.
I can't wait to see you in your *carrito*, hot shot. I'll be there
next month. *Con cariño*. Grandpa Benny."

Right away Teresa took it outside. Everyone admired her car.
The bikes parted when she pedaled down the sidewalk.

When a sharp-looking *ranfla* rolled by on the street, her neighbor Jóse Luis honked at her.

"I like your ride, *muchacha*," his voice cooed.

"I like your bomb *también*!" Teresa yelled in return.

The next day she paraded her car at the playground car show.

"Hop it!" the kids screamed.

Teresa hopped her car.

"Make it dance!" the kids screamed. *"¡Baílelo! ¡Baílelo!"*

She made it dance.

"Your car's a winner," the playground coach said.

"It's good-looking—*muy firme*."

Teresa drove away proud. When she got home, her father was in the driveway. Together they polished her car until the chrome was so bright it hurt their eyes. Teresa wouldn't let Pumpkin help.

"You can practice taking care of your trike," Teresa said,
"until you're big enough to have a *carrito*."

"I'm going to get me a *carrito* too," Pumpkin mumbled.
She cleaned her trike with an old diaper.

But one night Teresa left her little car out in the rain.

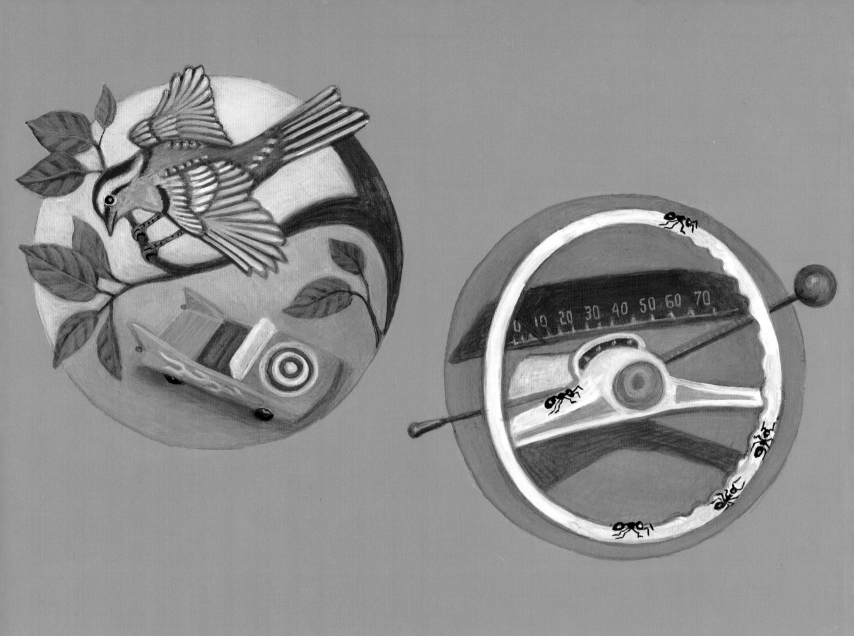

Another day she left it under a tree and a bird pooped on it.
Then ants attacked the steering wheel when it got sticky
from a soda. Even the flame stickers began to peel off.

"You should take care of your car, *mi'ja*," her mother
scolded. "You should know better. You're in first grade now."

ne day Teresa left her car in the driveway. Her father's truck backed into it.

"You could have been hurt," he huffed, glad that his daughter had not been in the car.

"It's all messed up!" Teresa cried. "Now it's going
to drive crooked."

"Could I have it?" Pumpkin begged. "I still like it."

Teresa ignored Pumpkin and rode away down the street.

As she went by one house, its screen door slapped open.
A dog as large as a cow barked at her.

"*¡Híjole!*" Teresa screamed. She spun her car around and took off as fast as a real car. The loose fenders rattled. The steering wheel vibrated like a washing machine, and a few of the stickers blew off.

"Faster," she yelled to her car.

Teresa pedaled until her legs burned. She thought she saw real flames leap from the tires.

"That was close," Teresa said, out of breath. "Thanks for saving me, *carrito*."

She patted the door where the stickers were peeling off. "I'm going to fix you up."

The next morning Teresa got to work. She was trying to straighten a crooked wheel when Grandpa Benny arrived.

"What do you have here, *mi'ja*?" her *abuelito* asked.

Teresa frowned. Her grandfather didn't even recognize the beautiful car he had given her.

"*Es mi carrito*," she answered softly.

Grandpa Benny propped his hands on his hips.

"*Pues*, it looks older than me," her grandfather said.

"Ready for the scrap heap."

Teresa examined her grandfather.

"You're not so old," Teresa said.

"Yeah, you still have hair, Grandpa," Pumpkin said.

"You got a lot in your ears."

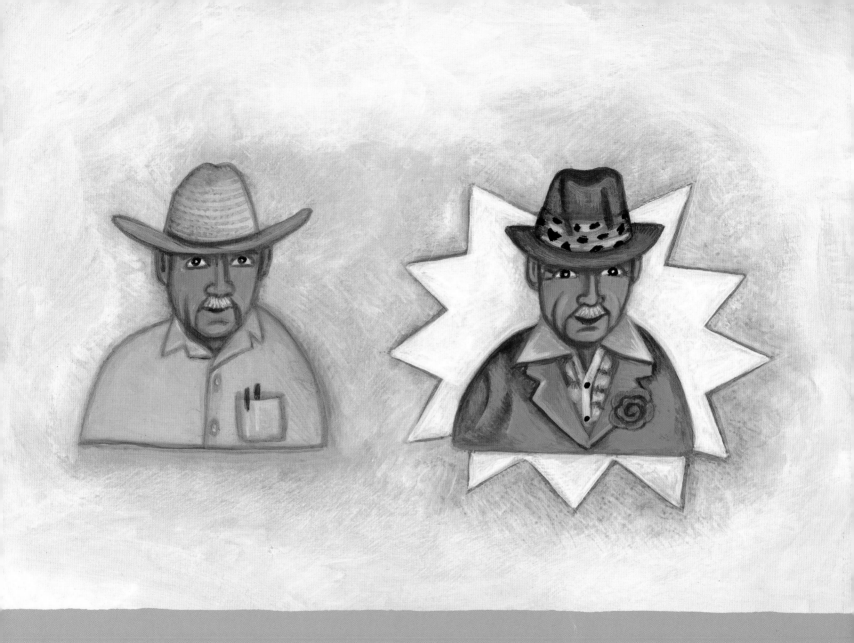

"Just like *mi carrito*!" said Teresa, and she told her grandfather that the dog almost caught her too.

"I still look pretty sharp when I'm fixed up," Grandpa said.
"Maybe we can fix up your car."

But Grandpa chuckled. "*Sí, es la verdad.* Guess I'm not so old, and I can run if I need to. Just now a dog chased me up your street. You should have seen me go!"

Abuelito led Teresa into the garage for the toolbox. They worked on the car until it looked sharp again. Teresa let Pumpkin sit in the car and wiggle the steering wheel like she was driving.

"The final touch!" *Abuelito* crowed, showing her
a special gift.

"You'll have the only lowrider with *chile* headlights."

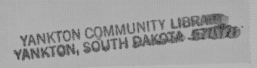

"Race you around the block," Teresa said.

"Why hurry?" Grandpa said. "Let the people see your beautiful ride."

"Sure," Teresa agreed. "Let's take it low and slow. Now *mi carrito* is better than ever, Grandpa. Just like you."